More Adventures With the Perfectly Pesky Pet Parrot

Julius
Again!

W9-CYC-464

VeraLee Wiggins

Pacific Press Publishing Association
Boise, Idaho
Oshawa, Ontario, Canada

Edited by Aileen Andres Sox
Designed by Dennis Ferree
Cover and inside art by Mary Rumford
Typeset in 14/17 New Century Schoolbook

Library of Congress Cataloging-in-Publication Data:

Wiggins, VeraLee, 1928-
    Julius again : more adventures with the perfectly pesky
pet parrot / VeraLee Wiggins.
        p.   cm.
    Summary: Amid the antics of his pet parrot Julius, Mitch
must cope with his mother's remarriage and the fact that
his bird has found a mate.
    ISBN 0-8163-1239-7
    [1. Parrots. 2. Pets. 3. Marriage. 4. Christian life.] I. Title.
PZ7.W6386Jt   1995
dc20   94-29438
                                                    CIP
                                                     AC

95 96 97 98 99 ● 5 4 3 2 1

Dedication

For you, Justin and Jeffrey.
I hope you wiggle and jiggle and giggle
while Mommy reads this book to you.
I love you much, much.
God loves you even more!

Other books by
VeraLee Wiggins

Contents

Julius hopped to

the top of Mr. Dewey's head.

"Am I in danger?"

Mr. Dewey asked.

CHAPTER

1

Mr. Dewey Meets Julius

"Mom," Mitch Sinclair called, "Mr. Dewey's coming over to talk to me tonight about a Sabbath School class hike, OK?"

Mom, in her bedroom changing, yelled through the door. "Sure," she called, "we'll just have to come home early." Her sister, Maxie, and Maxie's husband, Lloyd, had invited Mom and Mitch over for Sabbath lunch. Mitch's cousin Cassie and he always had fun together.

"Sure," Julius, Mitch's parrot, mimicked in exactly the same muffled voice Mitch had heard coming through the door. "Sure. Sure. Sure."

Mitch laughed. "Did she really sound

that bad?" he asked.

Mitch's best friend, Julius, extra large for a parrot, wore neon green feathers with a flaming red head and yellow cheeks. Only when he flew did he display the peacock blue feathers in his wings. Uncle Daryl had given the bird to Mitch about six months ago, when he got transferred to Baltimore, Maryland. Ever since then, Julius had been getting Mitch either into or out of trouble.

"Mom, can we take Julius to Cassie's?"

Mom came out of her bedroom, looking happy. "I don't remember them inviting Julius." She grinned at Mitch. "I guess you want Maxie to have a scalloped dining-room table like ours," she said. The first night they had had Julius, he had chewed the edge off Mom's new walnut table; he had chewed up a lampshade the same night. Not a good start. But he did better now that he knew Mom and Mitch.

Julius stayed home, and Mom and Mitch returned right after sunset so they wouldn't miss Mr. Dewey.

Mitch and Mom had barely finished studying the Sabbath School lesson when the doorbell rang. Mitch answered the door.

After inviting the man in, he turned to Mom. "This is my teacher, Mr. Dewey. Mr. Dewey, my mom."

The two spoke; then Mom asked Mr. Dewey about the hike.

"We're climbing Gobbler's Knob," he said. "Really, just—"

The loudly ringing doorbell interrupted. Neither Mom nor Mitch made any move toward the door. After several rings, Mr. Dewey asked. "Aren't you going to see who's there?"

Mitch and Mom giggled. "We already know," Mitch said.

A strange look crossed Mr. Dewey's face, as if he couldn't believe anyone not answering the door. "You aren't going to open it, then?"

Mitch laughed again. "That's right, Mr. Dewey, we're not."

"It's not like you think," Mom said, giggling. "We're really not that rude. Did you notice that bird sitting on the back of the chair over there? That's who's at the door. He's a copycat. Ringing the doorbell is one of his acts. He's also a telephone, and he copies perfectly the voice of anyone who interests him."

Mr. Dewey brightened. "Hey, that's quite a pet, Mitch. I hadn't heard about him." He got up and eased toward the parrot. "Let me get a look at this big guy."

Suddenly, Mitch got worried. Julius had really chewed Mitch's arms up when he first came to live with Mitch. "Uh—you'd better not do that," he said. Just as he said it, Julius hopped to the top of Mr. Dewey's head. He didn't bite or scratch but just sat grasping the man's hair with his claws. His bright head stuck way out, his face pointing at the man's. Julius didn't miss a move Mr. Dewey made.

"Am I in danger?" Mr. Dewey asked.

"I don't think so," Mitch said. "I'll get a date from the kitchen." A moment later he handed Mr. Dewey the small fruit. "Hold your arm out so he can sit on it while he eats," Mitch said. Two seconds later Julius sat on Mr. Dewey's forearm, crunching one of his favorite treats.

"He's a neat bird," Mr. Dewey said. "Why don't you bring him to Sabbath School?"

Mom laughed that time. "He already did," she said. "I guess you weren't around yet. Julius flew into the top of the church and sang louder than the congregation. Then he flew down and snatched Pastor Arden's glasses, took them up, and sawed them in two." She giggled as she remembered. "I don't think Julius would be welcome at church anymore."

"He's welcome in my Sabbath School class."

Just then, Julius flew to Mitch's shoulder. Scooting toward Mitch's face, he leaned against his cheek. *"Kkkkk, kkkk, kkkk,"* he said. Then he tweaked Mitch's lips.

"Did he bite you?" Mr. Dewey asked.

Mitch shook his head. "No, he kissed me. He thinks I'm his mother."

"That's not what the book says," Mom said. "Julius thinks Mitch is his wife. Parrots love their mates a lot and transfer that love to their keeper, if the keeper is good to them."

Julius kept whispering into Mitch's ear and kissing him. "Julius is tired," Mitch soon said. "Say good night, Julius."

"Good night, Julius," the bird repeated

in an exact imitation of Mitch's voice. Mitch took the parrot into his bedroom and opened the door of the big cage in the corner of the room. The bird hopped in, and Mitch locked the door. Then he wound up a small piece of wire around the door to keep Julius from leaving while he and Mom slept.

When Mitch returned, Mr. Dewey and Mom each sipped a cup of cranberry tea. "Shall we get busy on the hike stuff?" Mitch asked.

Mr. Dewey grinned and set his mug on the kitchen table. "Your mom and I just got it all figured out," he said. "We'll take along a camp stove and make burgers. We'll have picnic beans and potato salad. She even offered to make the potato salad. Eggless. Does that sound good, Mitch?"

"Yes. What else can we have?"

"How about watermelon?" Mom asked.

"Just the thing," Mr. Dewey said. After visiting for some time, he got up. "Well, this has been my best evening for over a year, but I better go before you put me in a cage and hang a blanket over it." As he talked he reached into his shirt pocket, then the other one, then several pockets in his pants.

"Hey, I seem to have misplaced my pen."

Mitch's stomach felt strange. "Was it bright and shiny?" he asked.

"Yes, silver and red. I got it for my birthday, and I better not lose it."

"We'll keep an eye out for it," Mom said.

"I really enjoyed meeting you, Fay," Mr. Dewey said. "After all the help, you'll go on the hike, won't you?"

"It's been fun meeting you too, Dan," Mom said. "And I'd love to go. Thanks."

Mr. Dewey left, and Mom turned to Mitch with sparkling eyes. "Hey, you didn't mention your Mr. Dewey was young, handsome, and nice," she said in an extra-happy voice.

"He's nice, but he isn't young."

Mom laughed. "He's young to me," she said. "Is he married?"

"I don't know," Mitch said. "And I don't care, either." When Mitch went to bed a little later, he had some new thoughts to sort out. Mom had acted almost like a girl who had seen a cute boy. Mitch didn't remember Dad, who had died when Mitch was two. But he wasn't at all sure he wanted Mom to act like that.

Julius landed on Cassie's arm

and buried his entire head

in her piece of watermelon.

CHAPTER

2

Julius Enjoys a Picnic

The next morning Mitch found Mr. Dewey's new red-and-silver pen stuffed under the tablecloth. "Poor Julius," Mitch said. "You never get to keep any of the neat things you find." That gave him an idea. "Do you have anything shiny that Julius can keep?" he asked Mom at breakfast.

She started to shake her head, then smiled. "Think he'd like my old key chain? It has only the old Honda key on it."

"Yes! He'd love it. Where is it?"

She got it and handed it to him. "Go ahead, give it to him."

Mitch shook his head. "Not until after school. Then I'll let him find it."

Mom dropped Mitch off at school on her way to work at the hospital.

All day in class Mitch thought about Julius's new toy. Much later, he greeted Mom. She always came home about the same time Mitch did. Then he ran to his bedroom, grabbed the key chain, and shoved it into his T-shirt pocket. The key dangled out.

"Heavenly sunshine, heavenly sunshine," Mitch sang as he opened Julius's door. "Hallelujah, Julius is mine." He'd started singing the song when he first got Julius. Sort of his way of thanking Jesus for giving him such a special pet.

The big bird hopped onto Mitch's shoulder. "Let's get you a date," Mitch said, hurrying to the kitchen. As he walked, the key jangled up and down outside his shirt pocket. Julius cocked his red head both ways, then leaned forward off Mitch's shoulder, still hanging tightly to Mitch's shirt with his feet. He snatched the key with his beak, then leaned back on the shoulder. Mitch didn't miss a step.

Mitch couldn't see what Julius did with the chain and key, but he heard it clanking beside his ear. The next instant Mitch heard a whir of feathers as the big bird headed to his perch above the drapes.

"What did you do with the chain?" Mitch asked. But he didn't see it again that day. When he finally found the key, he put it away for later.

Sabbath came, and right after church Mitch's class, with Mr. Dewey and Mom, started up the small but steep hill called Gobbler's Knob. Julius sat on Mitch's shoulder.

As the kids climbed, they sang "Do, Lord." All seven verses. "Wow, I must be out of shape," Mom said, puffing along.

Mitch didn't say anything, but he felt a little breathless too. "Do, Lord, oh do, Lord, oh do remember me," Julius sang lustily from his shoulder.

"Hey, no fair," Cassie, Mitch's cousin, told Mitch, puffing. "You aren't tired."

Mitch laughed. And puffed. "Too tired to sing."

"Heavenly sunshine, heavenly sunshine, hallelujah, Julius is mine."

"I suppose that wasn't you either, Mitch," Jodi, a girl who hiked near Mitch, said.

Mitch stopped. So did everyone else. "That was my parrot singing," he announced. "He can sing or talk in anyone's voice."

Everyone expressed amazement, then started climbing again. "OK," Jodi said, "we'll just see." She sang two verses of "Do, Lord," then asked Julius to repeat it. He sat on Mitch's shoulder as quiet as a stone. As heavy too, Mitch thought, even though birds have hollow bones to make them light for flying.

"He really does all this, kids," Mr. Dewey said, "but he does it when *he* chooses. Also, keep shiny things out of sight. He picked my pen from my pocket the other day and hid it under the tablecloth." He turned to Mitch. "Did I thank you for returning it? My niece would be very upset if I lost it."

Finally, they reached the summit, and Mr. Dewey pulled a one-burner camp stove from his backpack and lighted it. Mom put a skillet on it and plopped in some meatless burgers. In just a little while the eight kids and two grown-ups gathered about the loaded picnic table. Mr. Dewey asked God to bless them and also the food.

Then they began eating.

After about five minutes, Mitch heard the familiar whir of wings.

"Help," Jodi yelled, "that parrot stole half my bun."

Sure enough, Julius sat on a low limb with the bun in his left foot. His heavy bill tore into the bun, and seconds later the last bit disappeared. Mitch laughed, passing Jodi the plate of burgers.

Julius didn't bother anyone else until the watermelon came out. He thought that watermelon was just for him. First, he landed on Cassie's arm and buried his entire head in her piece of melon.

"Mitch," she screamed, laughing, "look at Julius!" Cassie already knew Julius and thought everything he did was funny.

When Cassie moved too much to suit Julius, he moved to Mr. Dewey's arm and took large chunks from his watermelon. Finally, Mitch put Julius on the empty end of the picnic table with what was left of the two pieces he had started on. Then everyone ate in peace while admiring Mitch's mischievous pet.

After they finished eating, Mr. Dewey

pointed out the view. "We sure can see a lot of the world God created for us," he said, pointing to a blue lake with a green meadow behind it. Behind that stood a bunch of different-colored trees. He turned to Julius. "I'm sure you all thought of this bird as another special gift from God." Then they played three nature games.

Later, the kids thanked Mr. Dewey for the fun day. "Thank you, thank you, thank you," Julius yelled as loud as he could in Cassie's clear girl's voice. Then, "You're welcome, you're welcome, you're welcome," in Mr. Dewey's deeper man's voice.

"He really does talk in different voices," Jodi said. "I wish he would say something in my voice." But Julius didn't.

After the parents had picked up the kids, Mr. Dewey took Mitch and Mom home.

"You two will have to come out to my place one of these Sabbaths," he said as he drove. "I call it a farm, although I've never raised anything to sell." He stopped talking long enough to shift down at a corner. "But it's country and I enjoy it," he finished.

"Sounds nice," Mom said. "We would like to see it, wouldn't we, Mitch?"

"Sure. Julius might like it too."

Mr. Dewey turned into the Sinclair driveway and pulled the keys from the ignition. "I'm sure he would like it, Mitch. By the way, I have a big dog. Will Julius like her?"

Mitch and Mom both laughed. "He likes dogs," Mitch said. "To ride, I mean."

They told him about the time Julius rescued Mitch, Cassie, and Gram from two large pit bull dogs. "Please come in and have worship with us, Dan," Mom added.

After they read a story and the lesson in the *Primary Treasure* and repeated the Lord's Prayer together, the three played Sorry and ate fresh popcorn.

After they finished playing, Mr. Dewey left. But he returned in less than three minutes, looking flustered. "I can't find my keys," he said. "Maybe I lost them in the couch."

Mitch got that old familiar feeling. Those keys weren't in the couch. He pulled a chair to the drapes, kicked off his shoes, and checked Julius's favorite hiding place. Not there. They looked everywhere Julius might hide keys. Mr. Dewey's keys seemed to have disappeared. And he couldn't go home without them.

Julius took off and kept going until he

disappeared. Mitch was really worried.

"He doesn't know where he is," he said.

CHAPTER

3

Julius Runs Away

Mitch felt awful when Mr. Dewey couldn't find his keys. Somehow he felt responsible for whatever Julius did. But he couldn't always control his pet. Then he remembered Julius's key. "Hey, if Julius gets his key, he may put it with Mr. Dewey's," he said. So he got Julius's key from his bedroom and put it in his shirt pocket. In less than sixty seconds, Julius dropped to Mitch's shoulder. Ten seconds later he took off with the old Honda key.

Everyone watched, wondering if the parrot would lead them to Mr. Dewey's keys. Mitch followed the beautiful green bird to the end of the living room. Julius dropped to the floor beside the coat closet. Mitch held his breath as the silly bird shoved the key under the door, then turned and strutted off as if he'd just done something pretty wonderful.

When Julius had walked several feet from the door, Mitch rushed over and jerked open the door. There, side by side on the floor lay the two sets of keys.

The next morning Cassie came over, and she and Mitch played badminton on the lawn. After Mitch beat her twice, she decided to get down to business. "Just a minute," she said, laughing. "I'll be able to move around better without these shoes." She pulled off her white shoes and bright red socks, then grabbed the racket again. "Just watch me now," she yelled across the net.

She beat Mitch that time, but when she started to put on her shoes she couldn't find her socks.

"You know who got them, don't you?" Mitch asked as he helped her look. "They may be in the top of a tree by now."

They searched the entire yard, behind every tree and under every bush.

"I give up," Mitch finally said. "Julius has more places to hide things than we know." He started for the house.

They ran up the steps to the wide front porch. For some reason, Mitch glanced across the porch to the wide swing. "Hey!" he yelled, pointing to a bunch of soft red threads hanging over and around the swing. "Could that be your socks?"

It was, of course. Cassie gathered up the weblike stuff and took it home to show Mitch's Aunt Maxie, her mom.

"I didn't know socks were made from fine yarn—or whatever that stuff was," Mitch said later when he told Mom about it.

"Silly," Mom said. "All fabrics are made from something like yarn or thread."

A while later Mitch answered the phone. "Well, hello, Mitch," Mr. Dewey's voice said. "How are you after our hike?"

Mitch couldn't believe his ears. Mr. Dewey called him! Him! A kid! He must really like Mitch to be calling just to talk. "I'm fine, Mr. Dewey," he said, laughing and feeling fantastic. "How are you?"

"Just great." The deep voice sounded

extra happy for some reason. Then Mr. Dewey cleared his throat. "Uh, er, would your mother happen to be home, Mitch?" Mitch's happiness dropped into a pile at his feet. The guy didn't call him at all! Mitch called Mom, and her voice sounded happy too.

As Mitch walked off, Julius let out a loud laugh. "I'm fine," he added in Mitch's voice.

"Oh, shut up, you stupid bird," Mitch snapped.

When Mom got off the phone, she called Mitch. "If Gram can come over, Dan wants to go out for dinner tonight. Is that all right with you?"

Mitch didn't understand why they wanted Gram to go. Then it hit him like a loaded freight train. They wanted to go alone! Without him!

"I asked if you mind?" Mom's voice asked, floating through the fog Mitch was in.

"Why should I care?" Mitch growled.

Gram came, and Mom and Mr. Dewey went out. Not only that night but twice more during the week.

The following Sabbath, Mom, Gram,

Mitch, and Julius drove out to Mr. Dewey's farm for lunch. Mitch liked the place a lot. The enormous old farmhouse had been remodeled until inside it looked nearly new. Light gold carpet in the living and dining rooms turned to sunny yellow tiles on the kitchen floor. The many windows and light walls gave the place an airy look. He felt sort of—free in it. Julius inspected every nook and cranny before returning to Mitch's shoulder.

Mr. Dewey had the lunch all ready and warmed it, then set it on the table. "Wow," Mitch said, "your yellow-flowered dishes match your house."

Mr. Dewey grinned. "That's the plan, Mitch. I hoped someone would notice sometime."

After lunch Mr. Dewey took the group outside to tour the place. A small barn matched the design and color of the house. Sweet-smelling hay filled the loft. A huge green pasture behind it looked as if it went on forever. "Where's your horse?" Mitch asked.

"I don't have one right now. Do you like horses?"

"I don't know. I've never ridden a horse." Mitch hated to admit that fact.

"Shut up, you stupid bird," Julius said in Mitch's voice. Then he lifted into the air and kept going until he disappeared. Mitch forgot all about horses. He pointed into space where he'd last seen his pet. "Did you see that?" he asked.

"I saw," Mr. Dewey said. "But you turn him loose all the time, don't you?"

Mitch nodded. He blinked his eyes hard to keep the tears back. "But he doesn't know where he is way out here."

Mr. Dewey dropped an arm over Mitch's shoulders. "Sure he does. Let's go in and have some juice. He'll be back before you finish it."

Mitch barely took time to gulp his juice. "May I be excused, Mr. Dewey?" he asked eagerly. "I need to watch for Julius."

Mr. Dewey smiled. "Of course, you can, Mitch, but Julius is all right. I'm sure he's been out here before if you turn him loose a lot."

Sunset came and went, but Julius didn't appear. "I have some things I need to do at home," Mom finally said. "Dan could call us when Julius comes, Mitch." But Mitch couldn't bear to go without his best friend.

At midnight Mom insisted they go home. "I don't know why Julius isn't here," she said, "but we can't keep Dan up any longer."

"I'll listen for Julius," Mr. Dewey promised. "Want me to call you right away? Even if it's four-thirty in the morning?"

"I won't be asleep, anyway," Mitch said. "I know something's happened to him. He's never stayed away this long . . . and besides that, he's never been here before."

"Why don't we pray about Julius before you leave?" Mr. Dewey asked. "You know our Father in heaven loves animals. He loves you even more and wants you to be happy." Mitch, Mom, Gram, and Mr. Dewey knelt on his soft golden carpet, and after thanking God for His love and care, they each asked Him to watch over the big green parrot and send him back.

Then Mitch and Gram and Mom climbed into the car and headed back to town. Tears ran down Mitch's cheeks, but the darkness hid them.

Mitch discovered Julius

completely wound up

in Gram's ball of yarn.

CHAPTER

4

Julius
Breaks Free

Mitch couldn't remember another time when he didn't want to go home. He usually loved his house, but tonight Julius wasn't with him.

"Maybe we'll have to stop taking him everywhere with us," Mom said into the darkness as she steered the car toward home. "Maybe we're expecting too much of Julius."

"It's too late to think of that now," Mitch grunted. Just then, Mom turned into their driveway. Mitch climbed out of the car. No need to go in. He wouldn't sleep a wink. Not with Julius lost somewhere in the black night.

As Mitch plodded toward the house, he heard Cassie calling. "Hello, hello. Oh, Mitch." What was Cassie doing here after midnight? Maybe she'd seen Julius! He picked up his feet a little faster. As he ran up the stairs to the porch, he heard a whir of feathers and a big dark blob settled on his shoulder. "Hallelujah, Julius is mine!" rang out into the night air. Then Julius crowded against Mitch's face. "*Kkkk, kkkk, kkkk*," he whispered softly and tweaked Mitch's lips several times.

Finally, Mitch came to himself. Julius was all right! "Hurry, Mom!" he called. He felt too excited to talk, but he had to tell her. "Julius is home! He's tired and wants to go to bed." Later, as Mitch fastened the wire that kept Julius in his cage, he couldn't help it. "Hallelujah, Julius is mine," he sang. He called Mr. Dewey to tell him the news. Then he and Mom both thanked God for bringing Julius home safely.

Mr. Dewey took Mom out the next evening. Gram came over and stayed with Mitch. They fixed something to eat together; then Gram sat in the recliner. "I might as well make use of my time," she said, picking up her knitting needles.

That reminded Mitch of Cassie's undone socks. "Can you knit socks?" he asked.

She nodded. "Sure, it's easy, but you have to use three needles, sometimes four."

He told her about all the soft stuff that used to be Cassie's socks. "Maybe that's what you call unmaking a pair of socks," he said. "And the stuff he pulled from those little socks went all over the place."

"That bird's a lot of trouble," Gram said in a kind voice. Then she seemed to think hard for a moment. Finally, she nodded. "Dewey seems to have taken quite a shine to your mother."

"Why do you say that, Gram?"

Gram laughed as her fingers flew, making the needles clack. "Have you noticed how much time you and I are spending together lately? He's been taking her out several times a week." She rested her hands a moment and smiled. "I'm so glad for her," she said. "He's a fine man, and Fay's been alone for too many years."

"Oh, Mitch, oh, Mitch!" Mitch turned his eyes to the sound and discovered Julius completely wound up in Gram's ball of pink yarn.

"Oh, Julius," Mitch returned. "I'm afraid you're in big trouble." He looked Julius over and saw dozens of strands of yarn around the bird's body.

"Looks kind of pretty, doesn't it?" Gram asked quietly.

All this time Julius kept pleading, "Oh, Mitch, oh, Mitch."

Mitch looked at the bright green and pink colors on his pet and started laughing. "Gram, you're the greatest. I thought you'd have fried parrot for breakfast."

Gram smiled. "I would if I ate meat. How do we get him out of that mess? Are you brave enough to pick him up and unwind him?"

Mitch wasn't sure but didn't want to admit it. How could a guy be afraid of his best friend? And Julius had never hurt him since the first night.

As Mitch tried to think what to do, Julius stopped calling his name. Then he heard some loud noise, almost like scissors snipping. When he looked down, Julius was cutting the last few strands of yarn from his body with his sharp beak. A moment later, Julius stepped from the shimmering pile of hot pink stuff and hopped onto Mitch's shoulder. "*Kkkk, kkk.*" When Julius started tweaking Mitch's lips, Mitch knew his pet was ready for bed.

When he returned from putting Julius to bed, Mitch looked again at the million circles of hot pink yarn on the carpet. "I guess you can't use that stuff now," he said. "Does it cost a lot of money?"

Gram's needles stopped clacking. She smiled and shook her head. "I can handle the expense," she said softly. "That's a lot less of a problem than you have with that thing you just put to bed. But thanks for caring, Mitch." She knitted a few more rows, then looked up at Mitch. "I was impressed with how fast Julius cut that stuff off him. He was really wound up, and I don't believe it took him fifteen seconds to free himself. Did you notice that, Mitch?"

He nodded. "The vet told me he has a sharpener in his top bill that keeps the bottom one as sharp as a razor blade. I believe it, don't you?"

"I do now." Her needles started clacking almost as fast as Julius had cut the yarn.

Mitch picked up the short pieces of yarn, each about eighteen inches long, and tossed them into the garbage. Then he jerked them out again. Maybe Julius would like them to play with. No telling what he'd do with them. Mitch hung them from the top of Julius's cage and went to bed.

As he lay there he remembered what Gram had been saying when Julius pulled his caper. She'd been saying that Mom and Mr. Dewey were spending a lot of time together. Exactly what Mitch had been trying not to think about.

Two days later Cassie came home from school with Mitch. They finished their homework and played a game of checkers. After a long, hard game, Mitch had Cassie almost cornered. Just a few more moves, and it would be all over. Mitch felt pretty good because Cassie usually won.

He leaned on his elbows, thinking carefully before he made his move. He wanted to win as quickly and cleanly as possible. Then a whir, a flash of blue in the green feathers, and both checkers of Mitch's most important king took off—in Julius's claws.

"Bring those back here," he yelled. The bird landed on top of the drapes. "Bring them back, Julius," he pleaded. "I can't win without that king."

Cassie doubled over with laughter. "Go, Julius," she called up to the bird. Then she met Mitch's eyes. "Now, whose side is he supposed to be on, anyway?" She laughed merrily. "I guess we don't have a winner. Tough, Mitch." Mitch didn't answer.

Cassie got up from the table. "Is Gram coming over tonight?" she asked.

"I don't know," Mitch grunted. What Cassie really meant was, *Is your mother going out with that guy again?* And he didn't want to think about it.

She sat back down. "You know something's going on, don't you, Mitch?"

"Like what?"

"Like you may be about to have a stepfather."

The next time Mitch opened his eyes

he could see the shadowy shapes of the

trees—and Julius, sitting on his chest.

CHAPTER

5

Julius Is Afraid of Storms

Mitch kept thinking about what Gram and Cassie had said. Mom and Mr. Dewey were spending a lot of time together. And he might end up with a stepfather. It wasn't that he didn't like Mr. Dewey. He did. But if things changed, life might not be so great anymore.

One afternoon a thunderstorm broke loose with the fury of a train load of dynamite. "That's close enough to almost scare me," Mom said as they watched out the window. Lightning kept lighting up the entire neighborhood. The heavy crashes followed so close that Mitch knew the storm was almost upon them.

"I'm going to look out the door to make sure I put my bike in the garage," he told Mom. When he opened the door, he felt something brush his face, then saw Julius leaving the porch. "Julius!" Mitch screamed. "You get back here. That racket will scare you out of the country." Julius kept going. Mitch called a dozen more times, but Julius didn't come back. Finally, he closed the door.

"What are we going to do about Julius?" he asked Mom.

She shook her dark head. "I'm not sure. This will scare him a lot, but you can't make him come back. He can fly and you can't. Besides, it is very dangerous for you to be out in a thunderstorm." She gave Mitch a mini-hug. "Julius getting himself into that mess reminds me of how we do the same thing. God wants to protect us, but we take off on our own." She grinned. "Just like a dumb bird. Let's pop some corn and play a game of Yahtzee. He'll be back before we finish."

The storm ended, but Julius didn't come. Mitch's bedtime did. "Go on to bed, Mitch," Mom said. "You know he'll be back, so you shouldn't worry."

Mitch yawned. "But he'll have to sleep outside if I'm in bed. May I take my sleeping bag out to the swing and sleep there until he comes?"

Mom hesitated, then agreed.

The next time Mitch opened his eyes he could see the shadowy shapes of trees—and Julius, sitting on his chest. Mitch started to get up and take Julius into the house, when he noticed Julius had something in his beak. He took it and held out his arm. The big bird hopped on, and Mitch deposited him in his large cage. Mitch walked off to the tune of Julius's quiet twittering. Mitch grinned. With the sounds Julius could make, he was everything from a doorbell to a tiny little bird.

Mitch stepped into the living room and turned on a lamp so he could see what Julius had brought home. Snowy white trimmed with bright red. Two seconds later he recognized a cloth baby shoe—almost new. Mitch wondered how soon the owner would be there yelling at him.

That evening Mr. Dewey showed up for supper. Probably Mom invited him. Mom fixed a company meal, which Mitch enjoyed, even though Mr. Dewey's presence bothered him some.

After they finished eating, Mitch showed them the baby shoe, wondering what to do about it. "You could take it around the houses in the neighborhood," Mr. Dewey said.

That sounded like a lot of work to Mitch. Embarrassing too. But he decided he'd do it. Before he left, the doorbell rang. Not Julius, but the real doorbell. An upset-looking young woman stood on the porch. "I'm sorry to bother you," she said. "I've been all over the neighborhood looking for my baby's shoe. I thought maybe she lost it while I pushed her past here in her stroller yesterday."

Mitch grinned all over his face. "Is it white and red?"

The woman's face transformed from worry to joy. "You found it," she said, almost laughing.

Mitch got the shoe, and the woman went away thanking him over and over. "Was I dishonest not to tell her about Julius?" Mitch asked Mom and Mr. Dewey.

"Not a bit," Mr. Dewey said. "You didn't

tell her anything at all, and you made her happy. For all you know, she did lose it, and Julius found it on the sidewalk." Mr. Dewey grinned. "He's your pet, Mitch. Give him a little credit, OK?"

Mitch went into his bedroom to go over his spelling words for tomorrow. His teacher told him he should be getting A's every time. He knew all the words except two, so he worked on those two for ten minutes and put his book away.

Hearing voices in the living room reminded him of Mom and Mr. Dewey. What was happening, anyway? "Please, Father," he said out loud, "don't let something happen to ruin our lives. I know You love us and want the best for us. Thank You."

When he walked into the living room, Mr. Dewey and Mom pulled apart from a kiss. Mitch felt a dark curtain slam down in his head. Everything looked as dark as it had from the swing last night after the storm. He started to turn around and go back to his room.

Before he turned, a big green bird landed on top of Mr. Dewey's head. Mitch almost wished he'd pull Mr. Dewey's hair out. But

Julius let out a sound that made Mitch cringe even as far away as he was.

"Awk! Awk! Awk!" the bright bird screamed. He jumped up and down, spread his green wings, then repeated himself. *"Awk! Awk! Awk!"* At about a billion decibels.

He jumped and repeated his squawks several more times before Mom came to her senses. "Mitch!" she screamed between Julius's squawks.

Mitch ran to the kitchen for some dates, then back to Julius and Mr. Dewey. "Here, Julius," he said quietly, holding out the luscious fruit.

Julius fluffed out his wings and opened his mouth for another series of squawks. Without even thinking, Mitch shoved the date in. Julius's eyes opened wide in surprise. He hiccuped, then ate the date.

Mitch reached a wrist up to Mr. Dewey's head, where Julius still sat. "Come, Julius," he said as calmly as he could. Julius hopped on, then on down to Mitch's shoulder. A moment later he snuggled close to Mitch's face, whispering his *"Kkkk, kkkk, kkkk."* When he gave Mitch's lips a few tweaks,

Mitch moved to the bedroom. Julius jumped into his cage.

Mitch retraced his steps to the living room, expecting to find his mom and Mr. Dewey still standing where he left them, scared to death. But he found them sitting on the couch, laughing together.

"That bird sounded exactly like he did the first night we had him," Mom said. "I thought that stuff was history."

"I did too," Mitch agreed. "He must have been really upset about something." Then he remembered Mom and Mr. Dewey's kiss.

"I hope he's the only one upset," Mom said.

"Yes," Mr. Dewey said, "because we have something to tell you. We want you to consider it the greatest news ever, because that's what it's going to be to you."

Mom smiled almost shyly. "Come sit beside me, Mitch."

Mitch didn't want to, but he did.

"Dan and I have decided to be married," she said quietly as soon as he settled. "Our home's going to be happier than it ever has."

Julius swished

through the back door and

landed on the cake.

CHAPTER

6

Julius Wears Cake

Mitch couldn't move a muscle. Mom and Mr. Dewey getting married? How could this happen?

Finally, Mr. Dewey made a nervous sound, maybe a laugh. "Well, I hope you have something to say about it, Mitch," he said.

Mitch couldn't think of a thing to say. The silence grew long. And embarrassing. "When?" he finally managed to blubber.

Mom's happy laugh sounded relieved. "In about a month," she said. "We'll be moving to the country, Mitch," she went on. "You'll love it out there. It's almost like the new earth will be. You saw it. It's perfect for a boy."

Mitch did like Mr. Dewey's place. He felt free there and almost ready to fly like Julius. But what if Mom wouldn't like him as much anymore? Mitch soon asked to be excused and went to bed. This was getting too much for him. He sort of felt like squawking—just like Julius.

The next night, Gram and Mr. Dewey came for supper, and everyone acted as if it were Christmas or county-fair time or something. That's how excited and happy they seemed. Even Grandma.

"Think I'm safe around Julius?" Mr. Dewey asked. Then he and Mom told Gram all about last night. Almost. All but the kiss.

Gram had brought a big cake with the words *DAN and FAY* written across the cake with lots of roses and some small flowers formed into heart shapes. A pretty fancy cake.

After the meal, while they all ate the delicious cake, Mr. Dewey held up a hand. Everyone quieted. "As soon as I swallow this cake, I have two things to ask you, Mitch." He gave a couple of big swallows and cleared his throat. "I'd like for you to be my best man," he said. "Think you could do that for me?"

Gram spoke up before Mitch's head cleared. "Don't you think he should give Fay away?" she asked. "Since he's her son and all."

Mom shook her head and licked a big glob of frosting from her fingers. "No one's giving me away, Mom. Because I'm not going anywhere. I want it understood that I'll be the same person in the same place with a dear son to cherish. Anyway, I'm not property to be sold or given away." She smiled tenderly at Mitch, then at Mr. Dewey. Finally, her eyes settled on her mother. "And I want you to be my matron of honor, Mom. OK?"

After Gram said she'd love to, Mr. Dewey spoke again. "I wasn't quite through with Mitch," he said. "Mitch, do you think you could call me Dad? I'd really like that. If you'd like time to get used to it, that's OK. If you simply can't do it, how about Dan? But I'd much rather it would be Dad."

Julius saved Mitch from answering. While they talked, Julius swished through

49

the open back door and landed on the cake. Well, he thought he'd land on the cake, but even his small weight landed *in* the cake. There he stood, his legs and even part of his body encased in the cake. Discovering his problem, he decided to take off. But the harder he beat his wings, the more he got messed up. And the more he didn't go anywhere.

Everyone laughed until Mitch snatched his pet from the cake. Then he realized what he had done. He had grabbed Julius with his hands and held him tight. Julius hated that usually. But Julius hadn't done anything to him—yet. Not knowing what else to do, Mitch rushed into the bathroom with Julius and set him on the counter.

Julius stood there looking into Mitch's eyes. "What are you thinking?" Mitch asked the silent bird. Julius said nothing.

Mitch wiped a big hunk of cake from Julius's legs and held it before the bird's mighty beak. Julius carefully worked at Mitch's hand until he got most of it, including crumbs. Then Mitch, getting braver, pulled out a washcloth and washed Julius's legs and messed-up feathers with warm water. Julius acted as if he knew Mitch was helping him.

"Hallelujah! Julius is mine," Mitch sang at the top of his lungs. "Thank You again, Father," he murmured. "For bringing me Julius."

Just as Mitch finished, Mr. Dewey came into the bathroom with a tiny plate of cake. "Can he have this much more?" he asked. Mitch put it in front of the bird, who didn't have to be asked twice.

"I suggested to Fay that she put the rest of the cake into small plastic bags and freeze them for special treats for Julius," Mr. Dewey said with a grin. "I thought he might enjoy the cake more than we would now that he has stood in it." He went back to the dining room, and Mitch felt good toward the kindly man. He could have been mad that Julius wrecked the cake.

"Mom," Mitch said eagerly as he slid into his place at the table, "did you see what I did?"

"No," she said, giggling, "but I saw what Julius did."

"Mom, he let me pick him up without even biting me. He trusts me to handle his body now. Isn't that great? It's worth even losing the cake. Isn't it, Mom?"

Gram laughed softly. "We didn't need that cake, Mitch. Julius trusted his entire self to you, didn't he, Mitch? You could slip and drop him, though, couldn't you, Mitch? Think God could make a mistake?"

Mom and Mr. Dewey went somewhere after supper. Gram and Mitch watched "Wheel of Fortune." Mitch could barely think about the letters Vanna turned over with all the stuff going through his head. Mom was getting married. It was true. It was true.

"Hey," Gram said, waving her hand before Mitch's eyes. "Are you unhappy?"

Mitch shook his head. "I don't know, Gram. Don't you think we've been getting along all right without Mom getting married?"

Gram laughed out loud. "You have, Mitch. That's because Fay has sacrificed her whole life to raising you. All mothers aren't like Fay. Better be thankful. But one of these days you're going to grow up and get married. What about your mother then, Mitch?"

He hadn't thought about that. He shrugged.

"Besides," Gram continued, "Dan is going to be a good father to you. Haven't you noticed what a nice man he is?"

Yeah. Mr. Dewey *was* a good guy. Probably Mitch's favorite adult man in the world. He put his tired pet in its cage and fell into his bed. Drowsily he tried to think about his troubles. He knew he could trust God more than Julius could trust him. So why was he worrying?

His mind kept getting fuzzy.

Then he heard a tiny little *"Kkkk, kkkk, kkkk"* and felt a light tweak on his lips.

Mitch felt happiness pour over him. Then he sat straight up in bed. Julius was out of his cage! No telling what he would do in the night if Mitch didn't put him back in and wire the door. He plopped back on the bed and felt the beak tweaking his lips again. So carefully. So gently. He simply must get up and—and do something. But what? What? What was it he'd wanted to do, anyway? He couldn't remember anymore. He was asleep.

Julius landed beside the coat closet

in the entryway. He tried to look

under the closet door.

CHAPTER

7

Julius Helps With the Wedding

When Mitch opened his eyes the next morning, he had a feeling of dread. At first, he thought it was Mom's engagement. Then he remembered. Julius had been loose all night! The only time Julius had been loose before, he'd wrecked Mom's walnut table and a lampshade.

Mitch jumped out of bed and headed through his bedroom door. "Hallelujah, Julius is mine." The song came from his bedroom! He turned around and found Julius blinking sleepily from his perch in his cage. Maybe he had just dreamed about Julius coming to him. But the open cage door told the story. Mitch ran through the house looking for damage but found none. He strolled back to his room feeling happy. Julius seemed to be getting quite civilized.

Mom went out with Mr. Dewey several times a week, and they always shared Sabbath lunch. Then suddenly Mom and Gram were busy making preparations for the wedding.

"It's going to be simple," Mom said. "You, Gram, Dan, and I will make up the wedding party. And we've invited only a few of our closest friends and relatives."

Mom and Gram decided to make the flowers from silk. "It'll be a lot cheaper," Mom said, "and we'll have them to help us remember the happy day."

One evening Mitch came in from taking Julius on a walk to find Mom looking around the living room. "What's up?" he asked.

Mom turned to him. "Remember the pink flowers we finished last night? I'm sure we left them on the tray. We always do until the glue dries." She pointed to the empty tray. "You can see they're not there."

Mitch's first thought was Julius. But Julius had been with him almost all the time since he'd come home from school.

He didn't say a word but marched right to his bedroom with Julius perched on his shoulder. When he closed the door, he held up his arm, and Julius hopped on. "OK, Julius," Mitch said, "I know it's not fair to blame you for it, but—did you?"

Julius stood tall, looking Mitch in the eye. He shook his feathers and gave his wings an experimental flap. "Heavenly sunshine, heavenly sunshine," he sang in Mitch's voice, "hallelujah, Julius is mine."

Mitch couldn't help laughing. "So you think that settles it, huh?" he asked his pet.

"Thank you, thank you, thank you," Julius yelled.

Mitch looked around his room. No pink flowers. He moved into the living room and looked everywhere he could think of. No flowers. Then a pile of green feathers with a flash of blue passed Mitch's head. Mitch quietly followed his pet. Julius landed on the carpet beside the coat closet in the entryway. He laid his red head flat on the carpet, trying to look under the closet door. Then his left foot snaked under the door.

Julius was definitely trying to reach something. Mitch opened the door. There,

Mom's missing pink flowers lay on the floor just out of Julius's reach. Mitch also picked up a teaspoon and two red checkers.

"I should have looked there the first thing," Mom said. "I'm sure we'll both remember after this. How many trips do you think Julius made to shove the flowers under the door? Fifty?"

About a week later, someone left a wedding present on the entryway table. As Mitch hurried to school, he noticed how festive the silver paper and ribbons looked. He wished he felt that happy about the wedding. Later that night Mom and Mr. Dewey called him into the living room. They both wore strange looks. "What did I do now?" Mitch asked. "Or was it Julius?"

"I'm not sure," Mom said, "but one of you has been getting into things again."

She took Mitch to the entryway and pointed at the package. Mitch took a deep breath. Julius couldn't have done that! Not even Julius. The wedding paper and ribbons had been removed. Neatly removed. So neatly that they should be lying on the table all folded up. But they weren't. Just the white box sat on the table now.

It took Mitch about five seconds to make a dive for the closet door. Sure enough, sixteen million tiny pieces of silver paper littered the floor. Mitch didn't see any sign of the ribbon, but it was around someplace.

"You aren't mad about that, are you?" he asked. "Not after the really bad things he's done?"

Mr. Dewey laughed. "We're not mad, Mitch. He's a pretty smart bird."

Finally, the day came for the wedding. A Sabbath day. Mom seemed nervous and jittery. Gram seemed superexcited. Mitch didn't know how to feel.

Mom and Gram had gone to the church Friday afternoon to decorate it so the church members could enjoy the flowers too. At seven o'clock Saturday evening, Mom and Mitch and Gram went to the church together. Mitch met Mr. Dewey and the pastor in the pastor's study.

When the organist started playing softly, Mitch followed Mr. Dewey onto the platform with the minister; then Gram and Mom came down the aisle and onto the platform beside the men.

Then, almost before it began, the wedding ended. Mom was married! Her name wasn't Sinclair anymore. Mitch felt strange. And alone.

Only about a dozen guests attended the simple wedding. They went back to Mitch and Mom's house afterward for a buffet supper.

"May I let Julius out?" Mitch asked Mom when they got home.

When she shook her head, Mitch noticed a million stars in her eyes. She was really that happy! He went back to the bedroom to stay with Julius and think about Mom. How could he feel bad when she looked as if she'd swallowed all the candy in the world? "Have You got things under control, God?" he asked out loud. A feeling of peace passed over him. He wished it would last.

Mr. Dewey took time to talk to Mitch that night after everyone left. He told Mitch that they would move to the farm tomorrow and put this place up for sale, if that was all right with Mitch. Mitch couldn't believe the man was asking him. Really, he knew he'd love the farm. "What about Julius?" he asked.

"Your room there is bigger than this one," the man said. "Seems to me, Julius will be happier. He'll have a bigger house to roam in and lots more space outside." He got to his feet. "My top priority is to make you and Fay happy," he said. Then he grinned. "Next on the list is Julius. He has to be happy too."

The next day Gram, Mom, Cassie's mother and dad, Mr. Dewey, and Mitch packed like crazy. About the middle of the afternoon, Mr. Dewey brought a U-Haul truck, and the group loaded it quickly. Everyone seemed so happy that they had lots of energy. Mitch tried to feel happy too.

By evening the old house looked empty. And Mr. Dewey's house looked like a big mess. Where would they ever put all the stuff?

Finally, Mitch put Julius into the big cage in his much bigger bedroom. He noticed the bright pink yarn pieces still hung from the top of the cage. Maybe some things hadn't changed. "This may just turn out all right," he told his pet while he wired the door shut. "If you'll like it here, I will too."

Before long the two parrots sat together on the same limb, giving each other the same kind of "Kkkk kkkk kkkk" that Julius gave Mitch. Mitch got a strange feeling in his stomach.

CHAPTER
8

Julius Finds a Friend

Mitch woke up the first morning at the farm wondering where he was. But when he heard Julius saying, "Thank you, thank you, thank you," he remembered. Jumping out of the comfortable bed, he ran through the box-strewn living room to the kitchen, where Mom and Mr. Dewey busily worked on breakfast. They looked so happy.

When Mitch finished breakfast, he took Julius outside to look around. Julius sat on his shoulder while Mitch checked through the barn. Pretty neat. Warm too. When they came out, Shawna, the big German shepherd, bounded up to them. Julius sat a few seconds, watching the dog approach, then took off flying.

"Come back, Julius," Mitch yelled. "You know you're not afraid of dogs. Julius, you come back here!" But Julius grew smaller and smaller until Mitch lost sight of him. He ran to the house.

"Mr. Dewey!" he said breathlessly. "Julius left! He's going home!"

"He'll be all right," Mr. Dewey said in a caring voice. "We'll wait about a half-hour, then go get him. Maybe you'd better keep him fastened to you for a little while, Mitch." He laid down his dishcloth and moved to Mitch. "Julius is OK," he repeated, dropping a big hand onto Mitch's shoulder. "I have another little problem," he added. "I don't know too many kids who call their fathers Mr. Do you, Mitch?"

Mitch grinned and shook his head.

"Have you given any thought to my suggestions?" He had asked Mitch to call him Dad. If Mitch couldn't do that, maybe he could call him Dan. Mitch had thought about it a lot, but it hadn't seemed right to call his Sabbath School teacher anything but Mr. Dewey.

"Yeah. I guess I could call you Dan.

At least, I'll try."

Mitch thought for sure Mr. Dew—Dan looked disappointed, but a moment later he smiled. "Great," he said. "Great for now. Now, do you think we should go after that runaway? I'm sure he'll be sitting on the doorknob at your old place trying his best not to fall off. And he'll be yelling at the top of his lungs."

And that's exactly what they found Julius doing. When he saw Mitch, he couldn't get close enough to his face with his little "*Kkkk, kkkk, kkkk.*"

As they got back into the car and started to drive away, Mitch noticed a For Sale sign in the front yard. *God*, he asked silently, *why do things have to change?*

Mom had stayed at the farm to start putting things away. "Where are you going to put all the stuff?" Mitch asked when they got back.

"We're not sure," Mr. De—Dan said. "Fay got all of your things into your bedroom. We decided to use my bedroom furniture. That's all we have figured out. Come on, I'll take you to school now."

Later, after school, Mitch took Julius

outside again. This time he put a piece of yarn around Julius's foot. He'd learned long ago that Julius wouldn't fly with yarn on his foot.

He took Julius out to the little orchard of apple, cherry, peach, and plum trees. "We've moved to a pretty neat place, Julius," he said, stroking the bright red head beside his face.

Just then, Mitch saw something in an apple tree that looked greener than leaves. Slowly he moved closer until he saw it better. A big bright green bird. He moved a little closer. Yes! It was a parrot! About Julius's size but not as pretty. It looked green all over. Julius's bright red head and yellow cheeks brightened him a lot. *What was a parrot doing loose in Dan's orchard?* Mitch put his hand on Julius's back to steady him and tore off to the house as fast as he could run.

"There's a green parrot in an apple tree!" he yelled as soon as he got inside.

Dan came out of the kitchen laughing. "No, there isn't, Mitch. He's right there on your shoulder."

Mitch cast a quick glance at Julius.

"No, Dan, a different one. Come see it."

Mom and Dan went out. Sure enough, the big bird still fluttered through the leaves, not seeming very wild. The three watched it for a while. Dan took Mom's hand. "Let's go call the Humane Society and also the park aviary. Someone's probably feeling pretty bad right now."

The aviary hadn't lost a parrot, but a man from the Humane Society came out and tried to catch the bird. Nearly unafraid, it kept just out of their reach. When the man brought out a fishing net, the parrot fluttered into the top of the tree, where they couldn't reach it.

"Do you think it's hungry?" Mitch asked that night after supper.

Dan shook his head. "Not now. There are all kinds of things out there for it to eat. But when it gets cold, it will be hungry." He laid down the paper he'd been reading. "I put ads in both of our city's papers," he said.

"What if you don't get a response?"

"I'm not sure. Let's hope the right person sees the ad."

Early the next morning Mitch took Julius and hurried to the orchard. After a little searching, he spotted the big bird sitting in the very top of a tree, soaking up the sun. After a few minutes, it spotted Mitch and started squawking just like Julius used to. That got Julius's attention in a hurry, and he lifted off Mitch's shoulder. A moment later he sat on a limb high in the cherry tree. He began squawking too. Mitch put his hands over his ears. Two squawking parrots was almost too much, even outside.

Mitch sat down in the lush grass between the trees and watched. Both birds hopped through the leaves, under and over the branches, squawking all the time. Suddenly, a horrible thought popped into Mitch's head. What if the birds got into a fight? "Come, Julius," he yelled. After repeating it several times, he went after help. "Mom, Dan, Julius is in the tree with the other parrot, and they're squawking at each other!"

Dan hurried out to the orchard with Mitch. "Shh," he whispered. Then he gently pushed Mitch into the grass and sat beside him.

After watching a little while, Dan leaned

close to Mitch. "They aren't going to fight," he whispered. "They're just getting acquainted." As they watched, the two birds closed the distance between them and also their mouths. The loud squawking changed to soft twitters.

"I don't believe it," Mitch said. "They like each other."

Dan grinned. And said nothing. After another five minutes, he patted Mitch on the shoulder and walked quietly away.

Before long, the two parrots sat together on the same limb, giving each other the same kind of "*Kkkk, kkkk, kkkk*" that Julius gave Mitch. When they started tweaking each other's bills, Mitch got a definitely strange feeling in his stomach. He waited a little longer, then got up. "Come on, Julius," he called. Julius acted as if he didn't hear a single word. Mitch called several more times, although he already knew Julius wasn't going to come.

"Well," he said, bursting into the house a little later. "I guess we have two wild parrots now. Julius is through with me. Where's my lunch? It's time for the school bus."

Then Julius landed on Shawna's back.

"No, Julius!" Mitch screamed.

CHAPTER
9

Julius
Rides Again

"Oh, Mitch," Mom said, "Julius would never stop loving you. Never in a million years. He'll be back before you get home from school."

Mitch wasn't sure about that. And Julius stayed in the orchard all day. Mitch went to bed that night without his pet. This move to the country hadn't turned out at all the way he had hoped.

He hadn't fallen asleep yet when he heard a loud "Come, Julius! Come, Julius. Right now!" in his own voice. He climbed out of bed and out the front door. Julius landed on Mitch's shoulder and scooted toward Mitch's face until the soft feathers brushed his cheek. Then, *"Kkkk, kkkk, kkkk,"* just before the tweaking began.

Mitch carried the tired bird inside and let him into his cage. "You two-timing rascal," he scolded lovingly. "As soon as a pretty girl comes along, you forget all about me. Maybe tomorrow we'll just stay in the house." He put the cover over the cage and crawled into bed.

The next morning Mitch found Mom and Dan at home again. Mom sat on the living-room floor Indian fashion, and Dan, on his knees beside a big box. It looked as if they'd been pulling everything out. "How long do you two have off work?" he asked.

"Two weeks for me," Dan said. "I'm trying to talk your mom into quitting her job and relaxing. She's had her share of grubbing around at work."

Mom laughed. "You're tempting me, but I like my job." She rolled over and leaned against Dan. "I guess we'll just take it a day at a time. It's nice to have a choice, anyway."

"Come, Julius, come, Julius, now!" Mitch's voice screamed from his bedroom.

Mitch laughed but didn't get up.

"I take it you've been yelling at Julius a little," Dan said. The phone's ringing interrupted him. He got up and answered the phone across the room. Then he held it away from his head. A moment later he hung it up.

"I know who that was," Mom said, laughing. "If he'd been able to see you pick it up, he'd have yelled 'hello' in someone's voice."

Dan sat back down on his knees and signaled Mitch toward his bedroom. "You'd better get Julius out of there before he thinks you don't like him anymore."

Mitch barely got to his feet, when the phone rang again. He listened hard and signaled to Dan to pick it up. "Go ahead," Dan said. "It's your home too."

Mitch did. "I saw your ad in the paper this morning," a girl's voice said.

"Just a minute, please," Mitch said and handed the phone to Dan.

"Tell me what other colors your parrot has," Dan suggested after listening a moment. After a short pause, his mouth opened into a wide grin. "I'm sorry, but this isn't your parrot. Good luck, though." He turned to Mitch, who had Julius riding his shoulder now, and shook his head. "I don't think they lost a parrot at all," he said.

"How come you asked about colors other than green?" Mitch asked.

"Because if anyone's going to have a free parrot, it might as well be you," he said.

Mitch didn't answer, but he thought that was pretty nice of Dan. He and Julius went out to check the orchard. The wild bird sat in the very top of a walnut tree, enjoying the sun. When it saw Mitch and Julius, it flew down to a limb just above their heads.

Julius gave Mitch a quick tweak on the lips and took off to the same branch. This time the birds flew awkward circles around the trees, making some kind of soft sounds. After watching awhile, Mitch went back to the house.

"I'm sure Julius has forgotten all about our other house," he told Mom and Dan while they ate breakfast.

Surprisingly, the house looked all settled again in a few days, and Mitch began to feel at home. Shawna, the German shepherd, loved Mitch from the start. "She's just been wanting someone who'd run and play with her," Dan said. "I do some, but she has a lot more energy than I."

A week passed. No one claimed the parrot. Mitch couldn't decide whether he was glad or sad. Julius spent too much time with it, but he still spent time with Mitch too. And he insisted in sleeping in his cage in Mitch's room. With Dan's help, Mitch had put out a feeder for both parrots. "Not because they need it right now," Dan said, "but because they'll enjoy it."

One afternoon Mitch and Shawna raced across the front yard. First, Mitch would chase the big dog; then the dog chased him. Once as he chased the dog, a flash of green with a blue touch whirred in front of Mitch. Then Julius landed on Shawna's back. "No, Julius!" Mitch screamed as the dog tore across the lawn with the parrot aboard. He remembered the time Julius rescued him from some dogs. He'd ripped those dogs all up. But not Shawna! *Please, God, don't let him hurt her.*

"Julius, it's all right," Mitch yelled as he followed the bird and dog as fast as he could run. All he needed right now was for the other parrot to get into the act.

"No, Julius! No, Julius, no, Julius, no Julius," came at top volume from Shawna's back. Then Mitch noticed the parrot wasn't trying to hurt Shawna. He just clung to the dog's fur, getting a ride.

Mitch stopped running and dropped to the ground, exhausted. Julius stretched his wings and lifted off Shawna's back. Five seconds later he dropped onto Mitch's shoulder. "No, Julius, no, Julius," he yelled into Mitch's ear. Shawna stopped running, and Mitch could tell she wanted to come to him but was afraid of Julius. For the first time, he felt his love divided. He wanted to comfort Shawna. But he couldn't call her for fear Julius would do something.

Then Julius took off toward the orchard. "Come, Shawna," Mitch called. "It's all right now. You can come. Come on over here, Shawna." Finally, the dog came, and they had a good tumble on the lawn together. Mitch went into the house feeling great that evening. He really liked living on the farm. He liked Shawna too.

"I was just thinking," Dan said after the three of them cleaned up the kitchen, "how would you like to help me make a house in the barn for the wild parrot? That way it'll be warm when the weather isn't."

That sounded like fun. "Sure," Mitch said. "Julius might like it, too, while he's with the other one." The two worked in the barn together every evening for a week. The house was four feet square and about the same height. It had a roof about like a real house, except it was just plywood instead of shingles. They put several perches inside, some solid and some on little chains so the birds could swing if they wanted. When they finished, Mitch brought some hay from the loft to put on the floor of the huge birdhouse.

Two days later, Mitch and Julius checked the big parrot house in the barn and discovered some sticks in it. And the bright pink yarn from Julius's cage lay tangled among the sticks. Almost like a half-built nest!

Mitch noticed a lot more parrot food

disappearing than usual.

Julius was feeding Lady Bird!

CHAPTER

10

Julius and Dan Become Fathers

When Mitch saw the sticks in the big birdhouse, he wondered what Julius would do with them. So he put the big bird on the peak of the roof. "Thank you, thank you," Julius yelled, hopping right to the door and into the house. Mitch peeked inside and saw the silly bird rearranging the sticks as if he knew exactly what he was doing.

"Come on, Julius," Mitch called after a few minutes, "let's go in now. I'm hungry." The bird kept moving sticks. "I'm going, Julius." As Mitch hurried away, he heard sticks bumping around inside. Before he reached the house, Julius's little feet grasped his shirt shoulder.

"I'm hungry, I'm hungry," Julius yelled when they burst through the kitchen door.

Dan lowered the glass of water he'd been drinking, laughed at the bird, then finished his drink.

"*Glug, glug, glug,*" Julius yelled.

Everyone broke up laughing. Finally, Dan wiped his eyes. "Did I really sound that bad?"

"Yes," Mitch said, laughing. "He really did sound like someone swallowing, didn't he?" Mitch asked.

"He did," Mom said. "Now put him away and get washed up for supper."

The next day after school, Mitch checked the big birdhouse again. The nest still looked a mess, with different-sized sticks and pink yarn. But he couldn't believe his eyes when he found a bluish green egg in it. He ran to the house.

"You won't believe me," he said when he found Mom and Dan setting the table. "I just saw an egg in the parrot house."

"You saw what?" Mom asked.

Dan shook his head. "We don't have any chickens, Mitch. Could Julius have put a rock in there?"

"No . . . it was an egg. Too small for a chicken egg, too big for a bird egg . . . and bluish green."

A look of wonder came over Dan's face. "I think we'd better name that other parrot," he finally said.

Mitch got so excited he could hardly talk. "Do you think it's a parrot egg?"

"I don't know what else. Did you see the other parrot there?"

Mitch shook his head.

The next day Mitch found another egg. He knew he shouldn't touch it, so he looked around for the other bird. She wasn't in the barn. He wondered how many eggs she would lay. He hung on to Julius's feet so he wouldn't go into the birdhouse. He might eat the eggs, for all Mitch knew.

Two days later Mitch found the green parrot on the nest. She ignored him until he got really close. Then her feathers puffed out, and she squawked at nine thousand decibels. Mitch backed out of the barn.

Dan got home late that night with a pack of papers. "I just learned a lot at the library," he said. "First, there are more than three hundred species of parrots.

These two seem to be some variation of the Amazon lord parrots. Most of that kind lay two or three eggs, which hatch in about eighteen days. Mark your calendar, Mitch, and you'll have a pretty good idea when to start looking."

After the family ate supper, they played a game of badminton on the lawn. Julius took off with the shuttlecock (birdie) twice. Both times he headed for the barn and came back without it.

"At least we know where his new hiding place is," Mom said.

"Or else he's trying to impress his wife," Dan said with a grin. "I think we'd better find a name for her. It's kind of awkward to always call her 'that other parrot.'"

Tired from batting the birdie across the net, they all sat in lawn chairs in the shade of a big weeping-willow tree. "I don't know," Mitch said. "I didn't even name Julius."

"Want a suggestion?" Dan asked hesitantly.

"Sure. What is it?"

"I have a couple. Julius Caesar's wife's name was Cornelia. If we don't like that, how about Cleopatra, his girlfriend after his wife died? Or we don't have to go with history at all. After all, these are living birds."

Mitch agreed that a parrot who was about to be a mother needed a name. A really nice name. "Say!" Dan said eagerly. "How about Lady Bird? That was the name of a president's wife." Everyone liked that name. So "that other parrot" became Lady Bird.

As the days passed, Mitch noticed a lot more parrot food disappearing than usual. He followed Julius and learned his pet was feeding the mother. Mitch crept through the barn as if it were a church. He feared the mother bird might take off, and the babies inside the eggs would die. Or that she might try to eat him alive.

Sometimes Julius sat on the eggs, but usually he brought food to her.

After the eighteenth day, Mitch could hardly stand not knowing. But Lady Bird stayed on the nest.

"Hey," Dan said one day. "Do you think we should put a parrot feeder in the barn? And maybe a waterer? Julius is wearing himself out carting food back and forth."

So together they made a feeder that held several pounds. Then they quietly put it up in the barn away from the birdhouse. As they worked on the waterer, they heard the parrot making small, quiet sounds. Then Mitch heard something else!

"Listen, Dad . . . I mean Dan," he whispered.

After listening a few moments, Dan broke into a wide grin, then a soft chuckle. He nodded. "We're hearing your baby parrots."

They worked awhile before Dan had something else to say. "Something else I learned at the library the other day was that parrots need mates, and it's cruel to keep one alone. That's the way I was, Mitch. I needed my own family. I'm glad for Julius. And I'm glad for me."

That night, Mitch got to thinking about his mistake, calling Dan "Dad."

He wondered why he'd been so afraid of the changes in his life. The changes had all been good. No, not good . . . great. *Thank You, God. Why didn't I trust You to work things out for me?*

He not only had Julius, but Lady Bird,

and at least one baby. He had the best dog ever. Then he thought about all the nice things Dan had done for him since he'd lived here. And all the things he'd put up with. A real father couldn't be nicer. After they had read the lesson from *Primary Treasure* and prayed that evening, Mitch moved to the couch beside Dan.

"I think I did mean 'Dad' this afternoon," he said almost shyly. "You're a good dad, and I'm glad you married my mom."

Tears glistened in Dad's eyes as he reached for Mitch. "I can't tell you how glad I am to hear those words, son. I'll do my best to be a good father to you." He grinned. "And to Julius."

As the days passed, Mitch felt happier than he ever had in his entire life. He thanked God every day for bringing Dad into his life.

He checked the parrots several times each day, hoping to see the babies, but Lady Bird hid them.

"I'm never going to get to see those babies," he fussed one evening at the supper table. "Sometimes I wonder if that bird really has any."

Lady Bird was finally

off the nest and Mitch could see

the baby parrot!

CHAPTER
11

Mitch,
the Bird Tamer

Dad laughed when Mitch fussed to see the baby birds. "Those little birds are two weeks old now. Why don't you just lift Lady Bird off the nest and take a good look?"

Mitch sank deeper into his chair. "No way. I haven't forgotten how Julius chewed me up when we first got him." He shook his head. "I'll just wait, Dad. One of these days she'll have to get off the nest."

Julius came into the house every day, but he chose to sleep in the barn with Lady Bird. One day Mitch carried water to the barn to fill the waterer, and Julius hopped onto his shoulder, leaned against his face, tweaked his lips, and whispered his little "*Kkkk, kkkk, kkkk.*"

Mitch's heart grew almost too big to fit into his chest. He loved Julius so much, and Julius loved him, even while raising babies. "Heavenly sunshine, heavenly sunshine, hallelujah, Julius is mine." *Thank You, Jesus, for my extra-special pet.*

Then he heard a whir, and Lady Bird landed on the waterer ... not two feet from Mitch and Julius. Mitch felt his body stiffen, but he didn't move. The all-green parrot looked Mitch right in the eye . . . and kept on looking.

What's she thinking? Mitch wondered. "Nice little mommy," he said softly. "Nice little bird. Nice little . . ." Then he remembered! Those baby birds were in the nest, with no mother to hide them. If he could get over there before she did, he'd get his first peek at the babies.

Inching away from the waterer and Lady Bird, he hoped she wouldn't notice. When he had reached a distance of about five feet, he couldn't wait any longer. He turned, with Julius still on his shoulder, and tiptoed across the barn to the nest.

He almost held his breath when he saw one little bird, so light green it looked almost white. It looked so cute he could hardly keep his hands off it. Then he remembered there had been two eggs! He looked carefully around the baby to make sure another wasn't hiding under or behind it. No, there was only one baby bird. He eased to the door and ran for the house as fast as he could. Julius rocked back and forth on his shoulder but managed to hang on.

Mom had just gotten home from her shift at the hospital. "I saw the baby bird," he said breathlessly, "but there were two eggs. There's only one baby, Mom."

Mom dropped an arm over Mitch's shoulder. "Don't feel bad, Mitch. Sometimes eggs don't hatch. Just be thankful one baby is strong and healthy."

Mitch nodded. "Yeah. I am glad. Come see it, Mom."

But when they got back to the barn, Lady Bird sat in front of her baby, and they couldn't see it.

"What color is it?" Mom asked.

Mitch shook his head. "I'm not sure.

Some kind of green, I think."

"Is it all green? Or does it have a red head and yellow cheeks like Julius?"

He shook his head again. "I couldn't tell, Mom. I'm sorry."

She ruffled his hair. "Don't be sorry. One of these days we'll see it all we want. And the colors will get brighter as it gets older."

Mom was right. In another week Lady Bird strayed from the nest a lot, and Mom, Dad, and even Gram got to see the baby parrot any time they wanted. Its body turned a bright green like both Julius and Lady Bird. And before they knew it, the baby looked as big as Julius and Lady Bird. It hopped all over the bench the bird-house sat on and stared back at anyone who came to see it. Lady Bird stayed near-by, and she and Julius carried food to it. But she didn't seem worried about her baby anymore.

One day Mitch and Gram stood looking at the baby, who stared back and chattered at them as usual. It made a sort of combination of a chirp and squawk. Gram smiled at Mitch. "One of these days it'll fly. I think it's time you named it too. Or are you going to sell it?"

Just then, Julius landed on top of the birdhouse and looked down at his baby. "*Chirrauk, chirrauk,*" he said. If Mitch hadn't been watching, he would have thought for sure the baby said it. Mitch and Gram laughed at his crazy copycat bird.

Mitch hadn't thought about selling the baby bird. When Dad called them for supper, he asked about it. "I'd hate to see you take it away from Lady Bird and Julius," Dad said. "That would be like taking you away from Mom and me."

Mitch shook his head. "Thanks, Dad. I would really like to keep it. But what if we get a flock of parrots that eat all the fruit off the trees?"

Mom laughed. "Why don't we worry about that problem when it gets here? Right now, we have plenty of fruit for us and for our little parrot family."

After supper they tried to think of a name for the baby bird but couldn't. They didn't even know whether it was a boy or girl. Somehow they began calling the baby 'Chick.'

Chick started to fly a few days later. Mitch laughed every time Chick took off. He had never seen anything so awkward. Chick flew sideways, up and down, and almost crashed onto the cement floor several times. Julius sat on the birdhouse watching Chick.

"What do you think, Julius?" Mitch asked. "He's the worst flier we ever saw, right?"

Julius didn't answer but hopped off the birdhouse and flew out the barn door. Mitch followed in time to watch Julius fly sideways, up and down, round and round, then land on the grass in a heap. He had copied Chick exactly. A moment later he landed on Mitch's shoulder, whispering in his ear. Mitch patted his pet, thanking God for his funny friend.

As the days passed, Mitch noticed an electric blue flash of color in Chick's wings when he flew. Just like Julius's. One morning when Julius landed on Mitch's shoulder, Lady Bird landed on his head. Mitch stood so still he held his breath. If he didn't try to catch her, Lady Bird might not bite him. Julius inched against

Mitch's cheek, but Lady Bird jumped into the air and flew back to the barn, which had become all the parrots' headquarters.

One evening some time later Mitch heard "Hello, hello, hello" at the door and went to let Julius in. But when he opened the door, he found all three parrots lined up on the porch railing. Julius still yelled "Hello," and the other two chirped soft sounds.

"Hello," Mitch said, feeling uncertain. "Am I supposed to let all of you in the house?" he asked. He pushed the door open a little. "Dad," he bellowed.

"Shall I let them all in?" he asked when Dad appeared.

Dad laughed. "I don't think Lady Bird and Chick would come in if you begged them," he said. "But it's pretty nice that they're brave enough to come to the porch now. We can't call her 'that wild parrot' anymore. Why don't you invite them in and see what happens?"

Mitch opened the door wide. "Come on, Julius, it's OK. You can bring your family in if you want." Julius hopped to Mitch's shoulder. Chick hopped to the same shoulder beside Julius. Lady Bird sat on the railing and watched. When Mitch moved into the house, Chick couldn't get back outside fast enough. Then he and Lady Bird began a duet, calling Julius to join them.

Mom appeared from somewhere. "Your little flock of parrots is getting tame," she said. "But can you imagine what three parrots would do to a dining-room table? Or even a lampshade?"

They all laughed together as they went inside for worship.